JUN   2016

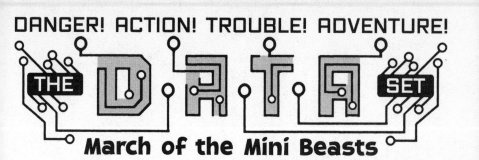

# DANGER! ACTION! TROUBLE! ADVENTURE!

# THE DATA SET

## March of the Mini Beasts

By Ada Hopper   Illustrated by Sam Ricks

LITTLE SIMON
New York  London  Toronto  Sydney  New Delhi

LITTLE SIMON

An imprint of Simon & Schuster Children's Publishing Division

1230 Avenue of the Americas, New York, New York 10020

First Little Simon hardcover edition April 2016. Copyright © 2016 by Simon & Schuster, Inc. All rights reserved, including the right of reproduction in whole or in part in any form. LITTLE SIMON is a registered trademark of Simon & Schuster, Inc., and associated colophon is a trademark of Simon & Schuster, Inc. For information about special discounts for bulk purchases, please contact Simon & Schuster Special Sales at 1-866-506-1949 or business@simonandschuster.com. The Simon & Schuster Speakers Bureau can bring authors to your live event. For more information or to book an event contact the Simon & Schuster Speakers Bureau at 1-866-248-3049 or visit our website at www.simonspeakers.com.

Designed by John Daly. The text of this book was set in Serifa.

Manufactured in the United States of America 0216 FFG 10 9 8 7 6 5 4 3 2 1

Library of Congress Cataloging-in-Publication Data

Hopper, Ada. March of the mini beasts / by Ada Hopper ; illustrated by Sam Ricks. — First Little Simon paperback edition. pages cm – (The DATA Set ; #1) Summary: "Three second-graders who love science get thrown in a wild spiral of adventures after meeting their reclusive neighbor, Dr. Gustav Bunsen. When Dr. Bunsen's growth ray hits a crate of animal figurines, the toys not only start growing, but also come to life" — Provided by publisher. [1. Science—Fiction. 2. Inventions—Fiction. 3. Clubs—Fiction. 4. Adventure and adventurers—Fiction.] I. Ricks, Sam, illustrator. II. Title. PZ7.1.H66Mar 2016 [Fic]—dc23 201500920

ISBN 978-1-4814-5729-3 (hc)
ISBN 978-1-4814-5728-6 (pbk)
ISBN 978-1-4814-5730-9 (eBook)

# CONTENTS

# Chapter 1

## The Data Set

Gabriel Martinez rang the doorbell. Then he, Laura Reyes, and Cesar Moreno held their breath.

Whoever came to the door would determine the fate of the world.

Or, at least, the fate of their school science club's field trip.

One of those two.

A woman in stretchy pants and a T-shirt answered. "What can I do for you three sweeties?"

*So far so good,* thought Gabriel. He quickly sized up the facts. The woman was in a friendly mood. *Good.* She'd called them "sweeties." *Excellent.* And then . . .

*Noooo!* On the television behind her blared an exercise program.

"One, two, three, four!" cried the instructor. "Chocolate won't rule you anymore!"

Gabe, Laura, and Cesar sighed.

Laura held up a box of science club fund-raiser chocolate bars. King-size. With extra nuts and caramel.

"Would you like to buy some delicious, um,

health-promoting chocolate? It's for our school science club. . . ."

The woman politely shook her head. "I'm afraid not, dear. I'm trying to be healthy." She patted her tummy. "But best of luck!"

The three friends plodded down the sidewalk.

"We're running out of houses," declared Gabe. "According to my estimates, we need to sell two more boxes to earn enough money."

Cesar unwrapped a chocolate bar and began to munch.

"Cesar, you're eating our chances of success!" Laura scolded.

"But I need to keep up my energy!" Cesar replied with a full mouth. Actually, because of the ooey-gooey caramel, it came out more like, "Buh I neef to keeb uh muh emergee."

Laura rolled her eyes. Cesar was always the hungriest member of the Data Set.

That was what these whiz kids from Newtonburg Elementary School were fondly known as: the Data Set. Gabe, Laura, and Cesar had gathered enough random facts and information—or data—to challenge even their brightest teachers, so the name stuck.

Gabriel was the oldest by two months, seventeen days, six hours, and three minutes. That made him the leader. He loved animals, big and small, and was fascinated by dinosaurs. If you had a question about dinosaurs, he could answer it quicker than you could say "Stegosaurus."

Laura was the team's engineer. It was hard inventing mechanical devices when you're only eight—Newtonburg

Home Improvement Depot doesn't exactly sell power tools to second graders. But Laura had a knack for making things work with rope, tape, bubble gum, and a bit of imagination.

And Cesar was the group's historian. He had a photographic memory and could remember all the dates, names, and facts from the page of a book simply by

looking at it once. He also had a big appetite. Usually this wasn't a problem.

*Unless* you were trying to sell chocolate bars to raise money so your school's science club could go see the sweet, sweet new neutron

generator on display in Teslaville. Then yes, a big appetite could indeed be a problem.

But against the odds and even a chocolate bar short, these three friends were optimistic.

"We can still do this, guys," Gabe

insisted. "There must be someone we can sell the last two boxes of chocolate to."

"Well," said Laura, "there is *one* more house."

She pointed down the street toward a teetering old Victorian. Rumor had it a strange man named Dr. Bunsen lived there. The dull-gray mansion loomed over the block, looking very out of place. Its shutters

hung at odd angles, and a twisted wrought-iron fence creaked in the breeze.

The three friends gulped.

Gabe squared his shoulders. "C'mon, guys," he said. "What's the worst that could happen?"

## Chapter 2

### Mad Dr. Bunsen

*Ding-dong!*

A tall, thin man with a mop of shaggy brown hair and gigantic magnifying goggles rolled back from his lab table. This was Dr. Gustav Bunsen.

"The doorbell?" he asked. "But I never get visitors."

He went to answer it. Outside were three children with monstrously large heads!

"Ahh!" screamed Dr. Bunsen.

"Ahh!" cried the children. The man had humungous eyes!

"Guys, relax," said Gabe. "It's just his goggles."

"Oh, right, these." Dr. Bunsen lifted his magnifying goggles. "I do

tend to startle myself each time I look in the mirror. Now, what can I do for you three, uh . . . ?"

"Children?" Laura finished.

"Right, children!" Dr. Bunsen rubbed his hands together. "I knew there was a word other than 'tiny humans.'"

The Data Set exchanged a look with one another.

"We're, um, selling chocolate," Laura said.

"For our school's science club," added Gabe.

"Wid exdra nuds." Cesar's mouth was still full.

"Chocolate?" Dr. Bunsen pulled a pair of tongs from his lab coat and plucked out a wrapped bar. He studied it. He sniffed it.

"I *love* chocolate!" he exclaimed. "I've been working for so long, I'd forgotten how much I enjoy a king-size bar. I'll take ten boxes."

"Ten?!" the three friends cried.

"But we only have two boxes left," Laura said.

"Oh." Dr. Bunsen frowned. "That is rather disappointing."

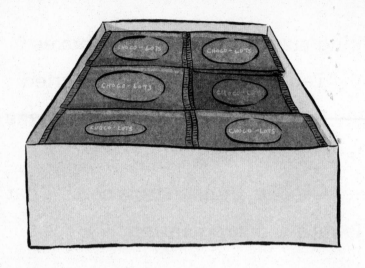

He studied the candy box in Laura's hands more closely. "Hmm, especially since this box appears a bar short."

Laura elbowed Cesar. Hard.

"But no matter!" Dr. Bunsen said. "Two boxes it is! Let me just grab some currency. Yes, currency is the name of the game. Especially when it comes to chocolate. King-size! With extra nuts!" His voice trailed off as he disappeared down the long hallway.

"*He's* a little extra nutty if you ask me," said Cesar.

"Nutty or not, now we'll have enough money for our field trip!" Laura smiled.

The three friends waited. And waited.

"Dr. Bunsen?" Gabe called. "Hello?"

They stepped cautiously inside.

Suddenly, Laura cried out.

"What is it?" Gabe asked, alarmed.

"Check it out!" Laura hurried into one of the rooms.

Her friends followed her . . . into the biggest scientific laboratory they had ever seen!

"That's a nanoscopic microscope," Laura exclaimed. "You can't get them outside of government research facilities. And this is a molecular field generator."

"How come we never knew this guy was so into science?" asked Gabe.

"Umm, maybe because he's a *mad* scientist," said Cesar.

Laura walked up to a very strange-looking contraption. "Hey, I wonder what this is. . . ."

"*That* is my latest invention." Dr. Bunsen's voice rang out behind them.

Gabe raised an eyebrow. "A growth ray? But that's impossible."

"Ah . . ." Dr. Bunsen wagged his finger. "That's what the National Science Academy said as well. But here it is! Which of you wants to grow first?"

"You want to test it on *us*?" asked Cesar. "That sounds . . . illegal."

"Here." Gabe came to the rescue. "Try it on Stego." He pulled out a small plastic Stegosaurus from his jacket pocket.

"But that's your lucky Stegosaurus," whispered Laura.

The three friends spun around. The doctor's eyes flashed. "Would you care to try it?"

## Chapter 3

### Growth Ray . . . Huzzah!

After a long pause, Laura broke into a wide grin.

"Would I?!" she exclaimed. "I love gadgets! What does it do?"

"Excellent!" Dr. Bunsen clapped his hands. He lifted the invention like a camera. "This, my young, 'snoopy' friends, is a *growth ray*."

"What if his machine melts it?"

"Better Stego than us," Gabe whispered back.

"Right!" Dr. Bunsen put on his goggles and used tweezers to grasp Stego. He gently placed the little dinosaur on the machine's platform. Then he picked up a handheld box with a flashing light and aimed it at the toy.

"Ready?" he asked. "Now stand back . . . and . . . huzzah!"

Dr. Bunsen pressed the box's red button.

The box whirred! It clicked!

It fizzled out. Nothing happened.

"Hmmmm," Dr. Bunsen said.

He pressed the button again and frowned. "I don't understand. My calculations are correct. It *should* work."

"It's okay, Dr. B." Gabe placed the very un-grown (and un-melted) Stego back in his pocket. "I read an essay last month that said growth ray technology is impossible. You didn't do anything wrong. It just can't work."

"Yes." Dr. Bunsen looked like he was near tears. "My old partner, Dr. von Naysayer, wrote that article. He knew I was working on this invention. And he said it was . . ." Dr. Bunsen's lower lip quivered. "Mad."

After a moment Cesar held out the boxes of chocolate. "Here, they're on the house."

"But our field trip!" Laura protested.

Cesar shook his head. "I think he needs these more than we do," he whispered.

And coming from Cesar, that was saying a lot.

## Chapter 4

## Laura's Super-Awesome Tree House

The next morning was a rare treat for the students at Newton-burg Elementary: a double teacher workday! That meant there was no school on Thursday or Friday. And when they weren't in school, the Data Set could be found in one place: their super-awesome, amazingly futuristic tree house that Laura designed.

Some kids had normal tree houses with ladders and wooden planks. That was cool. But the Data Set's tree house was unlike any other.

Laura had constructed it in

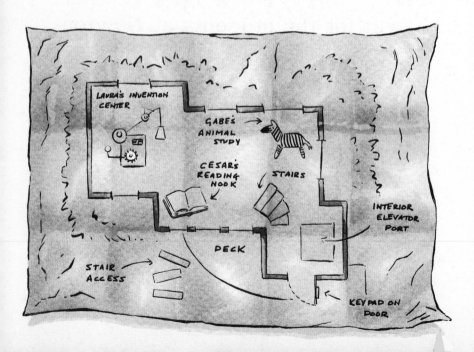

Gabe's backyard, high up in an old oak tree. The house was built out of welded scrap metal and high-density composite board. The windows had remote-controlled shutters. The door was guarded by a keypad lock. And best of all, Laura had rigged an elevator using a rope and pulley system. Why climb to the tree house when you could ascend to it—*in style*?

The sun shone brightly through the open windows.

Suddenly, a loud racket disrupted the quiet.

*Bang, clatter, clatter!*

"Cesar, can you keep it down?" Laura said without looking up.

Cesar huffed. "That wasn't me."

*Clatter, bang, sha-bing!*

"Cesar, please keep it down," said Gabe.

"I said it wasn't me!"

*Bump, thump, WHUMP!*

"What was that?!" Gabe and Laura exclaimed.

"See, it wasn't me!" Cesar said. Outside, a familiar voice cried out, "Whoooooaaa!"

The three friends poked their heads out of the window and saw a very upside-down and stuck Dr. Bunsen hanging from a tree branch.

"Dr. B.?" Gabe called. "What are you doing here?"

"Ah, yes, what indeed," the doctor replied. "I was coming to see you three, but I seem to have hit a snag."

Laura giggled. "Why didn't you use the elevator?"

The topsy-turvy doctor turned his head. "Ah—an elevator! How clever. I'm on my way!"

Soon Dr. Bunsen was safely inside. "I asked around for three inquisitive, slightly snoopy children and was directed here," he said, dusting off his coat. "People called you the 'Data Set'?"

Gabe smiled proudly. "That's us! What's up?"

"Well, after you left, I realized the mistake with my invention," the doctor explained. "I reset the flux generator. At last my growth ray is ready!"

The doctor whipped out the flashing box from his lab coat and pointed it at a small bucket in the corner of the tree house. It held several of Gabe's plastic animal toys.

"Observe!" he said. He pushed the red button. "HUZZAH!"

## Chapter 5

### Mini Beasts Alive!

Once again the box sizzled! It crackled!

*POOF!*

Still nothing. The plastic animals remained their normal size.

Gabe shook his head. "Dr. B., a growth ray would be cool. But I don't think it's going to happen."

The doctor was frustrated. "Hmm, but I *know* it should work!"

"It's okay," said Laura. "Sometimes you just need to— Ow! Cesar! You stepped on my jeans."

"Uh, I'm over here," Cesar said from across the tree house.

"Then who . . . ?" Laura looked down. Her eyes grew wide. A tiny, un-grown, but very much *alive,* miniature chimp was trying to

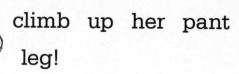

climb up her pant leg!

"A tiny monkey!" she cried. "You guys— check it out!"

The friends looked toward Gabe's tub of plastic figurines and gasped. The mini animals had all come to life!

One by one, they wobbled over like baby animals, looking for attention. A tiny elephant trumpeted when Gabe cupped it in his palm.

A teeny hippo waddled up to Cesar.
He plucked a tree leaf through the
window and fed it to the little hippo.
It munched happily! "Hey, guys, this
one likes me!"

Meanwhile, Laura marveled at a miniature giraffe. "Dr. B., the machine you invented is not a growth ray. It's a *life* ray!"

"Fascinating," said Dr. Bunsen. He picked up a pocket-size zebra. "I have no idea how this happened. I must study this further. May I please borrow this tiny zebra?"

"Sure," said Gabe. "But what should we do with the others?"

"We'll take care of them!" Laura exclaimed.

"Is that okay, Dr. B.?" Gabe asked.
The doctor shrugged. "They seem
to be quite happy." He gestured to

Cesar, who was feeding the hippo leaf after tasty leaf. "Just keep the animals together until I can figure out a way to return them to their normal, toy selves."

"Cool!" cried Laura.

"Come on, guys," said Cesar. "Let's grab Gabe's book on what animals like to eat. I can memorize these guys' favorite snacks."

"Speaking of 'favorite,' has anyone seen Stego?" Gabe suddenly asked. "I thought he was with the others, but I don't see him."

But the others were already on
their way down the tree-house
elevator and didn't hear him. Gabe
shrugged. He must have left Stego
inside the house somewhere.

At least, he hoped so.

# Chapter 6

## Wild Shenanigans

The friends spent the afternoon playing with their new pets! Laura used the empty fish tank to make a tiny terrarium. And Gabe helped Cesar skim his animal reference books for the perfect snacks for the mini beasts.

"They're so sweet!" Laura's

giraffe bounded over a small stick she held. "I wish we could keep them forever instead of turning them back into toys."

"Maybe we can ask Dr. B.," said Gabe. "They wouldn't be hard to take care of."

"Little Cesar Jr. doesn't want to go back to being a toy— do you, buddy?" Cesar said as he tickled the tiny hippo's tummy.

Confused, Gabe looked to the other side of the room . . .

. . . where the fish tank lay shattered on his bedroom floor.

"Uh-oh . . ."

The mini beasts were gone!

Gabe hopped carefully out of bed. "Mini beasts!" he whispered, tiptoeing down the hall. "Where are you?"

Laura rolled her eyes. "You named the hippo after yourself?"

Cesar shrugged. "Why not? It's an awesome name."

Soon the sun began to set. Laura gently placed the giraffe and the chimp in the terrarium next to Gabe's elephant. "See you first thing

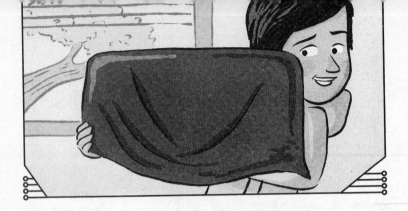

tomorrow to play with them?"

"Sure," said Gabe. "I'll watch them for the night."

"Call me if he starts to fuss," Cesar instructed. "I know what he likes to eat."

Gabe huffed. "*I* know what he likes to eat too. We looked it up together, remember? Anyway, see you guys in the morning."

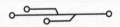

*Tink. Tink. Tink.*

Gabe opened one eye as sunlight peeked through his curtains. *Criiiiiiick. Craaaaaaaaack.*

Gabe rolled over in bed. "Just a few more minutes, Mom," he mumbled.

*SMASH!*

Gabe shot up. That sounded like glass breaking!

Soon he came to the kitchen. His mother was flipping pancakes while his sister, Juanita, bounced in her high chair.

"Good morning, *mi hijo*," Gabe's mom said in her pretty Colombian accent. "I'm making pancakes *con chocolate*. Would you like some?"

"In a second, Mom," said Gabe. He scanned the kitchen for the mini beasts. But all seemed normal.

Juanita suddenly started waving her arms and giggling. "Oooh, oooh, ahh, ahh!"

"Honey, could you see what Juanita wants?" Gabe's mom asked.

Gabe followed Juanita's eyes to the ceiling. Swinging from the light above his mother's head was the tiny chimp.

Except, it wasn't so tiny anymore. It was now the size of a pigeon.

Dr. B.'s invention had worked after all. The mini beasts were alive . . . and they were growing!

## Chapter 7

### March of the Mini Beasts

Gabe couldn't believe his eyes. His once pocket-sized toy was now a medium-sized chimp!

When his mom wasn't looking, Gabe tried to grab it. But the chimp swung out of his reach!

"Oooooh, ahh, ahh!" the not-so-mini beast cried.

"What was that, honey?"
Gabe's mom asked.

"Uh—I was just saying,
'Oooohh, ahh, can't wait for
chocolate-chip pancakes!'"

Gabe's mom smiled.
"*Bueno.* And there are
bananas on the table too."

*Bananas!* thought
Gabe. *Perfect!*

Suddenly, the chimp swung in a wide arc and accidently knocked over Juanita's sippy cup. Milk splattered all over.

"*Waaaaaaahhhh!*" Juanita cried.

"Oh, *chiquita*." Gabe's mom sighed. "Come on. Let's go get you cleaned up."

*Phew*, thought Gabe. *Saved by the spill.*

The moment they were gone, Gabe waved a banana for the chimp, and it eagerly jumped down.

"Gotcha!" Gabe cried triumphantly. "One down, three to go."

Gabe turned . . . and found Cesar Jr. lapping up the spilled milk.

He rolled his eyes. "Figures. Two down, two to go."

Just then the doorbell rang. It was Laura and Cesar.

Cesar crouched down by his hippo. "What did you feed Cesar Jr.? He's huge!"

"Dr. B.'s invention worked," Gabe said. "The mini beasts

aren't just alive. They're growing!"

"Where are the others?" Laura asked.

"I don't know," said Gabe.

"Stand by." Cesar stared off into space, scanning his memory for the pages on the giraffe and elephant.

"Giraffes like reaching for the tender foliage at the tops of trees. And elephants love water."

"The giraffe won't be tall enough to reach the trees," Laura observed. "It wouldn't reach much higher than, say . . ."

She pointed out the window.

"My mother's flower garden," Gabe finished for her.

The friends raced outside just in time to see the giraffe hopping to reach the low-hanging tulip leaves.

"He's jumping like I taught him!"

Laura grinned. Thinking fast, she waggled a tree branch in front of the giraffe. It jumped over it, right into her waiting arms.

"Now for the elephant," Gabe declared. "Cesar said they like water. And I know a place that's full of water *all* the time!"

He led his friends around the corner of the house to the birdbath.

Sure enough, there was the little elephant! Now the size of a small dog, it trumpeted merrily, spritzing water all over itself with its trunk.

In one quick motion Gabe

snatched the elephant from the birdbath. The elephant did *not* like that. It shot a spray of water right in Gabe's face.

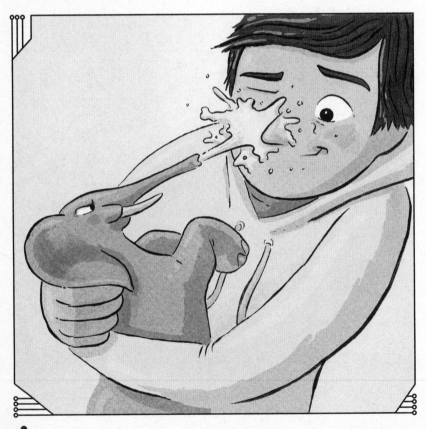

"You have a way with mini beasts," Cesar remarked.

Gabe sighed. "We have to find Dr. B. before they get any bigger."

Just then Gabe's mom stepped out onto the patio with Juanita.

"Gabe, will you watch your sister while I finish the pancakes?"

"Sure, Mom," called Gabe, hiding his not-so-mini beasts behind his back.

The moment Gabe's mom went back inside, Juanita began

laughing and pointing again.

"Uh-oh," said Gabe. "The last time she did that, she saw . . ."

"Puppy!" Juanita cried.

The friends looked where she was pointing and gasped.

Juanita hadn't spotted a puppy.

She'd spotted Stego racing across the lawn.

Dr. Bunsen's crazy growth ray had hit Stego, too!

# Chapter 8

## A Dino-Sized Problem

"Quick, grab him!" Gabe cried frantically.

The friends sprinted to catch the dino.

"It's slide tackle time!" exclaimed Cesar.

Cesar made a wild dive for the dinosaur . . . and Cesar Jr. slipped

from his grasp. Now the hippo was loose too!

"PUPPIES!" cheered Juanita.

"I can use your mom's garden hose to lasso them," Laura shouted.

She grabbed the rubber hose and tried to throw a loop around Stego's horns.

But the dinosaur's spikes pierced the tubing. Water sprayed everywhere, knocking the mini beasts from Gabe's and Laura's arms.

Now all five were on the loose!

Juanita squealed in delight. "AHHH!"

"Is everything all right out there?" Gabe's mom called from the kitchen.

Gabe felt like his head was going to explode. "Yeah, Mom!" he shouted.

"This is a disaster," he said to his friends. "What are we going to do?"

"Stand back!" a voice cried behind them.

Gabe turned just in time to see Dr. Bunsen racing into the backyard like a bizarre superhero, magnifying goggles in place and his white lab coat blowing in the breeze. He brandished a cannon-like machine with a net on the end.

The friends jumped back just in time.

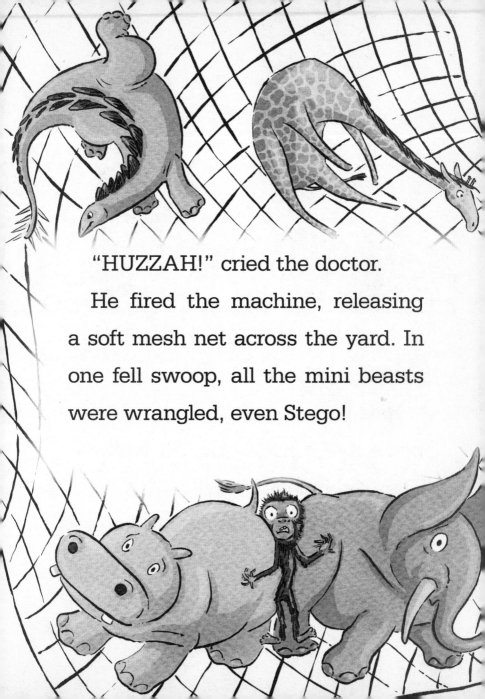

"HUZZAH!" cried the doctor.

He fired the machine, releasing a soft mesh net across the yard. In one fell swoop, all the mini beasts were wrangled, even Stego!

The Data Set sat on the lawn, panting, exhausted, and stunned.

Raising his goggles, the doctor broke into a huge grin. "It worked! They did indeed grow!"

Back in Dr. Bunsen's laboratory, there was a large pen for the beasts to scamper around in. Reunited

with their zebra friend, the not-so-mini beasts rolled and wrestled.

"Dr. Bunsen, did you figure out a way to fix this?" Laura asked.

"Alas, no," he admitted. "It seems the growth *and* life effects are quite irreversible. Based on my observations, the beasts will be full-size by tomorrow afternoon."

"What are we going to do?" asked Laura. "We can't raise real-life wild animals."

The doctor nodded. "Yes, it is quite a dilemma. I was hoping my three new—some might say 'snoopy'— friends would have an idea. Can you think of anywhere that might take care of exotic animals?"

"You mean a zoo?" Cesar joked.

Gabe, Laura, and Dr. Bunsen stared at him.

"Cesar, you're a genius!" Laura cried. "We'll take them to the zoo!

They'll be perfectly safe there."

Cesar blushed. Then he picked up one of the doctor's chocolate bars and took a bite. "What can I say? With great appetite, comes great brain power."

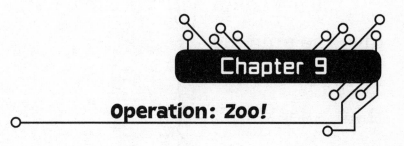

## Chapter 9

### Operation: Zoo!

The next morning four very ordinary-looking people pushed a very ordinary-looking stroller through Newtonburg Zoo. But underneath the pink blanket covering the stroller was a very, very *unordinary*-looking shape.

Cesar peeked beneath it. The

wide-eyed mini beasts stared back at him.

"Tell me again *why* we can't just give the animals to the zoo rather than sneaking them in?" complained Cesar.

"Because they'll want to know how we got ahold of a zebra, a giraffe, an elephant, a chimp, and a hippo," Laura explained for the hundredth time. "You can't adopt wild animals as pets."

"Or extinct animals," Gabe said, worried. "Dr. B., what are we going to do about Stego?"

"Never fear," said the doctor. "I have an idea that will keep your young dinosaur friend quite safe. But for now we have a stealth mission to complete!"

Gabe nodded. "Right. Cesar, are you ready with the zoo schedule?"

"You know it," said Cesar. He

had gone to camp at the zoo the past three summers and knew the animal-feeding routines by heart.

"Good," said Gabe. "Let's go over the plan. The workers open the pens to feed the animals on a set rotation each day. We'll use Juanita's stroller—modified to hold the mini beasts, thanks to Laura—to sneak our animals to the pen entrances. The workers will think the mini beasts wandered out and will take them into the pens."

"The elephants are first on the schedule," said Cesar. "That's where we should—hey! Don't touch that!"

A little girl was tugging at the pink stroller blanket. She stopped mid-pull.

"Sorry," said the girl's mother. "She just loves babies!

Do you mind if we take a peek at your adorable"—the mother eyed the unusual shape moving under the blanket—"bundle of joy?"

"No time, I'm afraid." The doctor stepped in. "Must be off. Animals to see, schedules to keep—oh, look! Another stroller!" He pointed, and when the mother turned, he and the Data Set zipped off!

At the elephant pen, the friends waited among the crowd of visitors. Right on schedule, the workers came. Stealthily, Gabe and Laura maneuvered the stroller to the pen entrance. The moment no one was looking, Gabe eased the little elephant out from under the blanket. It stumbled forward, bumping into the leg of one of the workers.

"Whoa!" The worker looked around, confused. "How did you get out here? Back into your pen with Mommy!"

"It worked!" Gabe whispered to his friends. "Come on!"

With the same sneaky skills, they returned the zebra, the giraffe, and the chimp. Last was Cesar Jr., the hippo.

The friends watched as the workers filed into the pen. But when
they turned to the stroller, they saw
Cesar Jr. looking up at them.

"Where's the blanket?" cried
Cesar.

The toddler from before was
standing next to the stroller clutch-
ing the blanket. Her mother stared
wide-eyed at the mini hippo.

"Is that . . . ?" she started.

"Gee, don't you just love your *stuffed* hippo?" Gabe exclaimed, shoving the tiny mini beast into Cesar's arms. "It's *so* funny how you push him in the stroller while Dad is changing our baby sister."

Cesar looked at the mother. "Yes," he said, deadpan. "I love playing with stuffed toys."

Before the mother could reply, the friends scurried away. Blending into the thick crowd, they quickly slipped alongside the pen entryway and nudged Cesar Jr. toward one of the workers.

"Well, hey there, little fella," the worker said when he noticed the tiny hippo. "You shouldn't be out here."

Happily, Cesar Jr. bounded into the pen with the other hippos.

Gabe, Laura, Cesar, and Dr. Bunsen stood with the now empty stroller, beaming.

"We did it, guys!" Gabe exclaimed. "We saved the mini beasts!"

## Chapter 10

### The Adventure of a Lifetime

The next morning the friends returned to Dr. Bunsen's laboratory.

"You never did tell me why you call yourselves the 'Data Set,'" Dr. Bunsen commented. "What does it mean?"

"Well, you see," began Laura. "We've gathered enough data—"

"It's an acronym," interrupted Gabe. His friends looked at him.

"It stands for 'Danger, Action, Trouble, Adventure!' It's kind of our thing."

"Yeah!" Cesar and Laura both exclaimed. "Exactly!"

Dr. Bunsen nodded thoughtfully. "In light of our adventure, I'd say that's an excellent description."

"But we still have Stego," Gabe pointed out. "Can we help him?"

A gleam came to the doctor's eye. "I believe I have the perfect invention for our dino dilemma. Follow me!"

The friends trooped after the doctor down the stairs of the mansion.

To their amazement, the basement held *another*, even larger laboratory!

"This is where I keep my prototypes," the doctor explained. "For years I've been working on a time-travel portal. It works, but I haven't had an opportunity to test it. I believe this is the perfect chance!"

"A time-travel portal?" Gabe repeated. "You mean we'll send Stego back to prehistoric times?"

"Precisely!" said the doctor. "Where he'll be with his own kind."

Gabe nodded. "I guess that is best." But he looked a little sad.

Laura placed a hand on his shoulder. "Think of it this way. Now Stego can be a real dinosaur. He'll be happier than ever!"

"You're right," Gabe said. He walked over to where Stego

waited in a large terrarium, built by the doctor, munching on banana leaves.

"Bye, buddy," he said. "I'm going to miss you. But you gave us the

adventure of a lifetime!" He looked to his friends. "Right, DATA Set?"

They smiled. "Right!"

"Okay!" said the doctor. "It's off to a prehistoric home for Stego!

And . . . *huzzah*!"

The doctor pressed a glowing button on the wall. In a bright green flash, the dinosaur vanished and was whisked away to the Jurassic period.

"Problem solved!" cheered the doctor. He waited for a response, but there was none.

"DATA Set?" he asked again.

The friends weren't there. The only thing the doctor saw was an empty laboratory. No dinosaur. No Gabe, Laura, or Cesar.

Small pops of electricity snapped from the time machine. The DATA Set were gone. "Oh, dear," said Dr. Bunsen to himself. "I suppose I should have told them to stand back."

# CHECK OUT THE NEXT DATA SET ADVENTURE!

*Fwoosh.* A hot breeze rustled through the jungle tree leaves.

*Screech!* A wild animal's cry echoed in the distance.

*Rummmmmble.*

"What was that?" Laura whispered nervously.

"That was my stomach," Cesar

admitted. "I should have eaten a bigger breakfast."

The friends rolled their eyes. But another wild animal cry rang out, and Laura, Gabriel, Cesar, and Stego the Stegosaurus huddled closer together.

"Guys," said Gabriel, "I don't think we're in Newtonburg anymore."

Gabe was right. These three whiz kids, known as the DATA Set, were indeed no longer in Newtonburg. The question was, where were they?